How Did You Grow So Big, So Soon?

For my sons, Will and Erik
—A. B.

For Tim—each day I am a better artist
and a better person because of you
—M. B.

Carolrhoda Books, Inc.
A division of Lerner Publishing Group
241 First Avenue North
Minneapolis, MN 55401 U.S.A.

Website address: www.lernerbooks.com

Library of Congress Cataloging-in-Publication Data

Bowen, Anne, 1952–
    How did you grow so big, so soon? / by Anne Bowen ; illustrated by Marni Backer.
       p.   cm.
    Summary: The night before his first day at school, a mother and son recount other new experiences he has had, such as his first words and first steps, and celebrate his growth and accomplishments.
    ISBN: 0–87614–024–X (lib. bdg. : alk. paper)
    [1. Mother and child—Fiction. 2. First day of school—Fiction. 3. Growth—Fiction.]
    I. Backer, Marni, ill. II. Title.
    PZ7.B671945 Ho 2003
    [E]—dc21   2002008317

Manufactured in the United States of America
1 2 3 4 5 6 – DP – 08 07 06 05 04 03

How Did You Grow So Big, So Soon?

by Anne Bowen
illustrations by Marni Backer

Carolrhoda Books, Inc. / Minneapolis

Climb into bed.
I'll tuck you in tight.
Tomorrow will be
your first day of school.

   I'm not little anymore, Mama.

How did you grow
so big, so soon?

Did you know me
when I was small?

I knew your heart first,
beating beneath mine,
a tiny fist curled
inside me.

What was I like,
when I was small?
Tell me, Mama,
one more time.

When you were born...

I was naked and tiny.

Yes, you were naked and tiny,
peach-rosy and smooth,
soft wisps of hair
all over your head.

Did I talk?

No, you blinked and blinked,
then you cried.

Was I loud?

Yes, you were.
But in my arms
you fell asleep,
tiny and warm and new.

What did I say first?

You said, "Ma-ma-ma."

That's YOU!

That's right.

Now I can talk
and sing songs
and tell stories, too.

How did you grow
so big, so soon?

Tell me again, Mama,
about the first time I walked.

*I held your hand
and you took one step,
then another and another.*

Did I fall?

You plopped down once,
trying hard not to cry.
But you stood up
and tried again.

Just like when I learned
to ride my bike!

*Now you can run
and jump and skip
to the park.*

I can swing by myself, too.
Higher than the trees,
higher than the porch,
higher than you, Mama!

How did you grow
so big, so soon?

What will I do
on my first day
of school?

You'll sing songs,
draw pictures,
and read books, too.

Just like we do, Mama.

But you'll do these things
with new friends at school.

What if I feel scared?

When you were small,
you were afraid of the dark.
Now Bear sleeps with you
and you're not afraid.

Can Bear come with me
when I go to school?
He can hide in my
backpack, Mama.
Bear will be VERY quiet.

Bear may go with you.
I'm sure he'll be quiet.

What will you do
when I'm at school?

I'll be thinking of you.

Who will you play with
all day when I'm gone?

Oh, I won't be alone.

Who will be here, Mama?

YOU.

When I see your shoes
on the mat by the door,
you will be with me.

When I picture your smile
and think of your hug,
you will be with me.

And when school is over
and it's time to come home . . .

. . . you'll be there, Mama,
waiting for me?

I'll be there waiting
to hear all about
your first day of school!

Now close your eyes,
tomorrow's YOUR day!

I'm not little anymore, Mama.

I know.
You're my big boy now.

*How did you grow
so big, so soon?*